HELEN HALL LIBRARY
100 Walker St
League City, TX 77573

DISCARD

D0573682

Feb 19

Ella & Monkey at Sea

Emilie Boon

CANDLEWICK PRESS

HELEN HALL LIBRARY
100 Walker St
League City, TX 77573

DISCARD

Monkey doesn't like good-bye hugs.
He doesn't want to say good-bye to Oma.
Oma wipes away tears and hugs Mama too.

"Come along, Ella!" Mama says to me.

"Papa's waiting in America."

"Come along, Monkey!" I say.

But Monkey doesn't want to get on a ship,
or sail off to sea, or move away forever.

Monkey doesn't like it when Mama
tucks us into tiny bunk beds.
He wants his own bed at home.

I sing him Oma's lullaby until he falls asleep.

In the morning, Mama takes us to the playroom.

Monkey doesn't want to play.
The teacher says we can just watch.
So that's what we do until Mama
comes to pick us up.

At dinner, Monkey tries to mind his manners,
which means being polite to the waiter,
and to the captain, who stops to say hello.
But Monkey misses Oma and dinners at home,
and he hates fish.

Every day, we go to the playroom.
Every day, the teacher asks us
if we'd like to play.
Every day, Monkey says no.

Monkey is getting grumpier.
The sea and wind are wilder.
The ship rocks harder, higher —
up, down, up, down — like a seesaw.

That night, Monkey doesn't feel like eating dinner.

His plate slides down the table.

His tummy feels funny.

So does mine.

Monkey doesn't want to roll
from side to side in bed
or listen to the wind howl.
He just wants to be home.
Me too.

Next morning, Monkey is clingy.

The sea and wind are wild, wild, wild.

Someone whispers, "Hurricane."

Everyone is sick.

The hallways are empty.

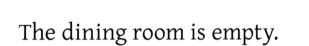

The dining room is empty.

The playroom is almost empty,
and there's nothing to watch.

So we try the crayons. I scribble with angry black. Scared gray. Cold blue. Bluer, grayer, blacker — until my crayons snap.

Then I borrow Monkey's crayons.
And I start a new drawing.

I draw and draw, until my hand is tired,
and Mama comes back.
She smiles when she sees my sun pictures.
I give her my favorite.

Monkey and I hand out pictures.
One for the teacher. One for the waiter.

The biggest sun goes to the captain.

On our last day, the sea is quiet.
The captain says my sun pictures saved the day.
Monkey and I draw pictures for Papa:
Tulips. Oma. The ship. And the trees in the
backyard Mama promises me in America.

That night, Mama takes Monkey and me
out to see the moon. I point to the stars.
Mama says they're the faraway lights
of New York — our new home.
Tomorrow I will see Papa again.

Finally tomorrow comes!
Monkey loves hello hugs.
So do I.

For my mother, who packed so many suitcases,
and for Oma, who knew how to create her own sunshine

Copyright © 2018 by Emilie Boon. All rights reserved. No part of this book may be reproduced, transmitted, or stored in an information retrieval system in any form or by any means, graphic, electronic, or mechanical, including photocopying, taping, and recording, without prior written permission from the publisher. First edition 2018. Library of Congress Catalog Card Number pending. ISBN 978-0-7636-9233-9. This book was typeset in Gentium. The illustrations were done in watercolor, graphite, colored pencil, and crayon. Candlewick Press, 99 Dover Street, Somerville, Massachusetts 02144. visit us at www.candlewick.com.
Printed in Shenzhen, Guangdong, China. 18 19 20 21 22 23 CCP 10 9 8 7 6 5 4 3 2 1

HELEN HALL LIBRARY
100 Walker St
League City, TX 77573